cl♣verleaf books™

Off to School

Sam Visits the School Library

by **Martha E. H. Rustad**

Illustrated by **Jess Golden**

Ṁ MILLBROOK PRESS • MINNEAPOLIS

For B, fellow bibliophile—M.E.H.R.

To Kelly—J.G.

Text and illustrations copyright © 2018 by
Lerner Publishing Group, Inc.

Millbrook Press
A division of Lerner Publishing Group, Inc.
241 First Avenue North
Minneapolis, MN 55401 USA

For reading levels and more information, look up this title at
www.lernerbooks.com.

Main body text set in Slappy Inline 22/28.
Typeface provided by T26.

Library of Congress Cataloging-in-Publication Data

The Cataloging-in-Publication Data for *Sam Visits the School
   Library* is on file at the Library of Congress.
ISBN 978-1-5124-3938-0 (lib. bdg.)
ISBN 978-1-5124-5578-6 (pbk.)
ISBN 978-1-5124-5107-8 (EB pdf)

Manufactured in the United States of America
1-42151-25424-1/24/2017

TABLE OF CONTENTS

Chapter One
Library Day

I get to visit the library today! My class goes one day each week. I am bringing back the book I checked out last week.

Our teacher, Miss Hill, leads us to the library.

Some school libraries are called media centers.

At the library, we return any books that we borrowed and read. We say hello to our librarian, Mrs. Lopez.

Another name for a librarian is library media specialist.

Mrs. Lopez is teaching us how to research animals.

She shows us a book and a website about sharks.

She knows how to find out anything!

Mrs. Lopez lets us try out our own research. Malik signs up to use a computer. He is researching ocean animals. He wants to know what whales eat.

Chapter Two

Picking What to Read

Now we get to look for new books to read! Zac looks at the nonfiction section and finds a book about planets. **Numbers on the shelf help him find the book he wants.**

NONFICTION
500 - 599

GEOGRAPHY

Nonfiction books have facts. Fiction books tell stories that are not true.

Amira is in the fiction section. She finds a mystery book about a missing pet.

Ben looks at the graphic novel shelves. He likes the way the drawings tell a story.

Vera uses headphones to listen to an audiobook.
Simone is reading an e-book. There are lots
of different ways to read books!

Chapter Three

Checking Out

I found a book with poems about animals. I bring it to the desk. Mrs. Lopez scans my card and the book.

It's checked out! Now I can go to the reading corner to look at my new book!

RETURNS

15

Skyler wants to read the next book in her favorite series, but she cannot find it on the shelf. Mrs. Lopez puts her name on the waiting list. Skyler will be able to check out the book when it comes back to the library.

Miss Hill says it is time to go back to our classroom. We have to check out our books and log off the computers. Then we say good-bye to Mrs. Lopez.

She reminds us to bring our books back next week.

When we get back to the classroom, I put my book in my backpack. I'm excited to finish reading it at home. **I love library day!**

It is important to take good care of library books so other people can borrow them too.

21

Find It!

Libraries have lots of information and many different materials. Play this game with your friends to find as many items as you can. Ask your librarian if you can play Find It in your library.

1) a nonfiction book

2) a chapter book

3) a picture book

4) a story about a dog

5) a graphic novel

6) a poetry book

7) a magazine

8) a mystery book

9) an animal book

10) a joke book

11) a book about another country

12) a science book

GLOSSARY

audiobook: a recording of someone reading a book out loud

e-book: a book you can read on a mobile device, a tablet, or an e-reader. Many libraries have e-books to check out.

fiction: a book that tells a story that is not true

graphic novel: a book that tells a story using comic strips

librarian: a person who works in a library. Librarians help people find information in books, magazines, and on websites.

library media specialist: another name for a librarian

media center: another name for a library

nonfiction: a book with information that is true

research: to find information about something

BOOKS

Cleary, Brian P. *Do You Know Dewey? Exploring the Dewey Decimal System.*
Minneapolis: Millbrook Press, 2013. Read this fun introduction to the Dewey Decimal System,
a system librarians use to organize library materials.

Lindeen, Mary. *A Visit to the Library.* Chicago: Norwood House, 2016. Read about all
the activities available during a library visit.

Meister, Cari. *Public Library.* Minneapolis: Jump!, 2016. Follow along as a class visits a
public library.

Parsley, Elise. *If You Ever Want to Bring a Circus to the Library, Don't!* New
York: Little, Brown, 2016. Read this fun, illustrated book to learn what not to do in a library!

St. John, Amanda. *How a Library Works.* Mankato, MN: Child's
World, 2013. Learn more about how libraries work and what you can find
at a library.

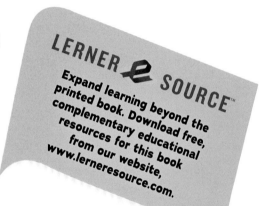

LERNER *e* SOURCE™

Expand learning beyond the printed book. Download free, complementary educational resources for this book from our website, www.lernerresource.com.

WEBSITES

The Dewey Decimal System
http://www.factmonster.com/ipka/A0768720.html
This site explains what different numbers mean in the Dewey
Decimal System.

International Children's Library
http://en.childrenslibrary.org
Find books for kids in many languages.